THE PRINCE AND THE MERMAID

The story of *The Prince and the Mermaid* first came to light through Gottfried Von Strassburg in the thirteenth century but the tale is, in fact, based on a much earlier French folktale called *Mélusine and the Prince*.

THE PRINCE
AND THE
MERMAID

IAN DEUCHAR

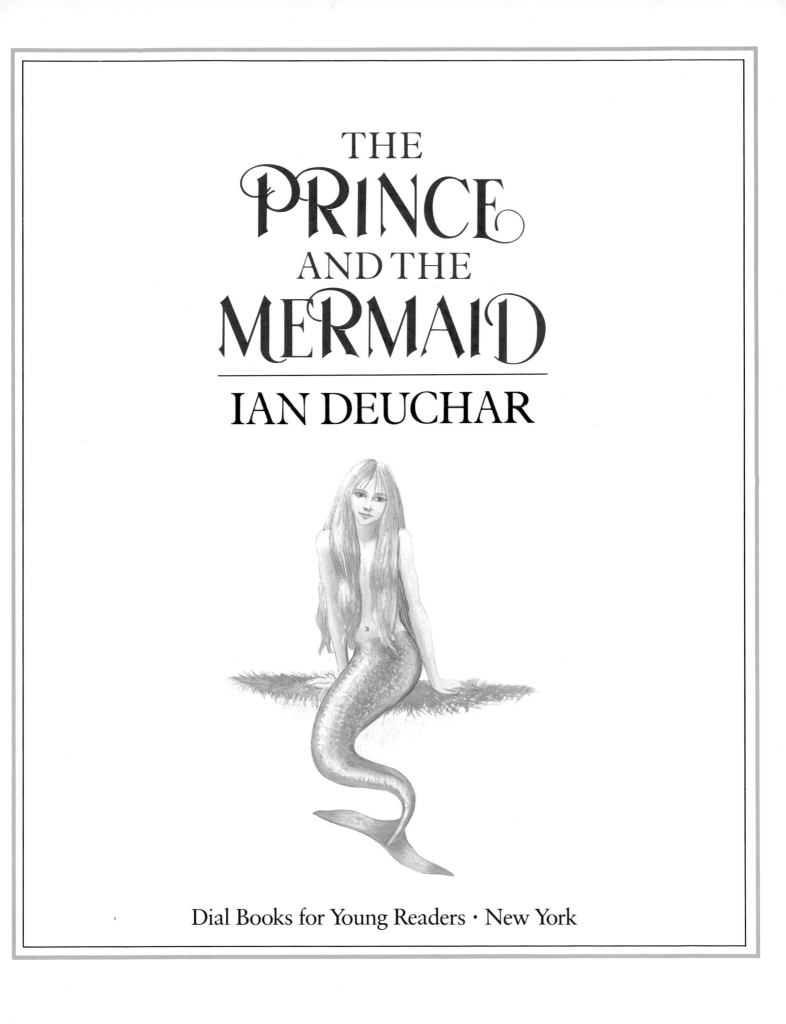

Dial Books for Young Readers · New York

It was snowing. The leaden sky gave promise of even more to fall. For weeks the mermaids had found no comfort, either freezing in the icy sea or shivering in the howling winds ashore. None of them could remember such a cold winter, and when icebergs appeared, the mermaids swam up an inland river for safety.

Deep upstream, the river flowed through an ancient forest, so thick and deep that even winter's icy grip could not reach inside. Here the mermaids found shelter until the first snowdrop petal pushed its way through the melting snow and it was time to return to the sea.

But one young mermaid stayed behind. She had grown to love the river that meandered through the forest. Floating among the reeds she saw the otters play and kingfishers dive. She watched the graceful swans glide by as she swam under a canopy of twisting trees. Sometimes she thought of her sisters in the far-off emerald sea and became sad. But her new friends in the river soon chased all sad thoughts away as they played around her.

One morning the peace of the river was shattered. The trees rang with the thunder of hooves and the cries of huntsmen, and the river creatures scattered in fear.

All day the forest echoed to the hunters' shouts as they chased the wild boar. The Mermaid was too terrified to move and hid, trembling, among the reeds as the hunters raged around the forest in pursuit of their quarry.

As evening drew on, the sounds slowly died away. The Mermaid was about to slide from her shelter when she froze. A figure on horseback had come down to the water's edge. He dismounted and led his horse to drink. The Mermaid's fear gave way to curiosity when she saw a handsome young man, so finely dressed he could only be a prince.

After that day, the Prince returned many times to the river, drawn to the spot though not knowing why, and the Mermaid longed more and more to talk to him. But since mermaids cannot talk to humans, there was only one thing she could do – use an ancient spell known only to mermaids.

By the light of the next full moon, she spoke the magic words and immediately turned into a beautiful young woman.

The next day she waited by the river until the
Prince arrived. He was astonished to see such a
beauty. Her long blonde hair tumbled over her
shoulders and she gazed at him with eyes of
sparkling sea-green. They met every day and, as the
summer passed, fell deeply in love. The Prince told
his father of the woman he loved so much. The king
said, "You must bring her to me so I can meet the
one who has captured my son's heart."

As the Prince led the Mermaid from the forest,
she saw a huge, splendid castle, its towers and
battlements gleaming in the sunshine. She was
overjoyed, but one fear troubled her. The Prince
must never learn the secret of her spell, for if he did,
the spell would be broken.

Taking his hand she said: "Swear me an oath, or
we can go no farther. Never ask from where I have
come or why I must return there at each full moon."
Although puzzled by her strange request, the Prince
readily agreed.

The whole court had gathered in the great hall to see the beautiful woman, jostling each other for the best view as the Prince led her to the king.

The king was enchanted with her and the whole court was delighted. In the excitement, no one noticed one lady who glared with hatred at the Mermaid. This lady had loved the Prince since they played together as children, and was sure that she would be the one whose hand the Prince would seek in marriage. The sight of the Prince's happiness was more than she could bear. She slipped quickly away in case anyone should see her eyes filled with tears.

On the day of the wedding, fanfares played and cascades of rose petals fluttered everywhere. All day and all night the people sang and danced in the streets until the dawn lit their weary but happy way home.

Time passed and the Mermaid gave birth to a baby boy. She and the Prince presented the little baby to the king and saw the old man's face light up with joy. He spent many hours with his new grandson, dreaming of the day when the child would inherit the kingdom.

But one person did not share the joy. The lady who had once loved the Prince now hated him more than ever, seeing his great happiness with another.

In the forest lived an evil witch, feared by everyone for her power. In an old crumbling tower she cast spells and spoke with Dark Forces. Shivering with fear, the jealous lady sought the witch's help to end the Prince's happiness.

The witch muttered strange words and peered deep into her seething cauldron. She saw the Mermaid's secret, but such was the goodness that shone from the Mermaid's heart, the witch was powerless to destroy her. In fury, she cast a spell over the Prince.

"You shall have your wish," hissed the witch to the jealous lady. "The heart of the one you loved shall be filled with doubt. Evil spirits shall whisper in his ear by day and fill his dreams by night."

As the witch shrieked and cackled, the jealous lady crept away, filled with dread at what she had now done.

Now the Prince spent little time with his wife and son, but stayed alone in his chamber. "What ails you, my love?" asked the Mermaid. "Where is the happy young man I married?"

The Prince glared at her. "Answer me this. Where do you go on the nights of the full moon? Why do you go alone into the forest?"

"You swore never to ask me. You promised. I cannot tell you," cried the Mermaid.

"Then go!" shouted the Prince. "If you will not tell me I'll speak no more with you. Go!"

As the full moon drew near, the Prince thought, I can stand this no longer. I must know where she goes.

A voice whispered in his ear, "She deceives you. Follow her. Forget your silly promise."

That night the Mermaid slipped out of the castle and down into the forest. It was quite dark and still save for the hoot of an owl and the rustle of leaves.

The Mermaid stopped still, certain she had heard a footfall, and whispered, "Is anyone there?" But there was only silence.

Slipping off her robe, she slid quietly into the river. Once again she was a mermaid, her scales glittering in the moonlit waters. She splashed and dived in the cool river until it was time for the spell to change her once more back to a human being.

She pulled herself from the river and then looked up in horror. There stood the Prince, his eyes wide with shock and alarm.

Hurt and angry, the Mermaid cried out, "Oh, why did you break your promise? I cannot stay now that you know my secret and have seen me in my true form." With a cry of despair she turned and dived back into the dark water.

It was a heartbroken Prince who returned to the castle. He had been selfish and foolish to break the trust of the one he loved. The whole kingdom mourned the loss of their Princess. Every day he watched from his window in the vain hope of seeing his Mermaid again.

The jealous lady sat beside him. "Do not be sad," she said. "Forget her. I can give you true happiness. And after all, it was hardly fitting for a prince of royal blood to marry a sea creature, a mere fish!"

"I would not have such a heartless creature as you," the Prince shouted. "How dare you! She shall return, never fear. Now go, I never wish to see you again."

Seasons changed, months became years and still he watched and waited, but the Mermaid never, ever, came back.

But every time the moon was full, the Mermaid became human and slipped quietly into the sleeping castle.

All night she watched her son sleeping peacefully in his little bed and, as dawn approached, she stole into the Prince's chamber and lightly kissed her sleeping love before returning to the river.

First published in the United States 1989
by Dial Books for Young Readers
A Division of Penguin Books USA Inc.
2 Park Avenue
New York, New York 10016

Published in Great Britain
by Methuen Children's Books Ltd
Copyright © 1989 by Ian Deuchar
All rights reserved
Printed in Italy by Olivotto
First Edition
N
1 3 5 7 9 10 8 6 4 2

Library of Congress Cataloging in Publication Data
Deuchar, Ian.
The prince and the mermaid.
Summary: The prince and the mermaid's happy
marriage is threatened when a wicked
witch casts an evil spell.
[1. Fairy tales. 2. Folklore—France.] I. Title.
PZ8.D477Pr 1990   398.2′1′0944   88-33395
ISBN 0-8037-0638-3